D0160582

To Dave
"The Storyteller"
Love,
Jeffie
1992

'Twas the Night After Christmas

Christmas

"The Untold Story"

'Twas the Night After Christmas

Christmas

"The Untold Story"

By
Jean Drake, Muffin Drake, Susan Pierce

Illustrated by
Robin Bielefeld

P PETER PAUPER PRESS, INC.
WHITE PLAINS · NEW YORK

Special thanks to my real "Mrs. Claus" — my Mom. My thanks also goes to the "Special Elves" whose help was required to bring this book into your hands — my supportive family — Tiffiny & Shannon. Thanks is also due to Terry McCue, book designer, without whose help Mrs. Claus would still be on the drawing board. Thanks also to Art Lackner for re-working all my mistakes!

— Jean

I dedicate this book to my own special Mrs. Claus, Genevieve Bowman Schick, the "tired" Mrs. Claus behind a sweetheart of a Santa, E.H. Schick, Sr. And, I dedicate this to Garrett E. Pierce, the most valued and loved Santa in my life who just happened to enter the lives of the Schick family on Christmas Eve, and to my two special not-so-little elves, Christopher and Garrett. And to E.H. Schick, Jr., Sally, Mary, and Sandy.

— Susie

Copyright © 1990 Jean Drake
Published by:
Peter Pauper Press, Inc.
202 Mamaroneck Avenue
White Plains, N.Y. 10601
(ISBN 0-88088-547-5)
Library of Congress No. 90-61144
Printed in Hong Kong

This Book is Dedicated to:

Mary Joan

and to All the Other Mrs. Claus
who for hundreds of years have done
it all and let Santa take the glory
for the magic of the holidays —
the festivities, traditions and
celebrations which do not come
about by sheer magic!!!

'Twas the night after Christmas
    and time for a pause;
Collapsed in the corner
    sat tired Mrs. Claus.
The stockings were empty
    the house was a mess;
The tree had tipped over —
    she couldn't care less!
Her muscles were aching,
    her feet were so sore,
This overworked lady
    couldn't take any more!

The elves were a-sleeping
      each tucked in his bed;
But visions and fantasies
      danced in her head!
She felt somewhat down
      and a wee-bit dejected
And thought this past year
      She had been so neglected!
Come next year no baking
      and trimming the tree —
On the beach with the elves
      is where she would be!

STARRING MRS. CLAUS

Then she envisioned
    a gorgeous new sable,
With emeralds and rubies
    hanging down to her navel!
When up on the roof
    there arose such a clatter;
It ended her dreaming . . .
    "Now, what is the matter?"
Away to the window
    she flew like a flash —
She tripped on the clutter,
    hopped over the trash.

And what to her weary-red
   eyes did appear?
But the emptied-out sleigh
   and eight hungry reindeer.
''Where's that little old driver
   so lively and quick?
Like a grammar school kid
   pretending he's sick!
Now Dasher, now Dancer,
   now Prancer and Vixen;
Here Comet, here Cupid,
   here Donner, and Blixen,

Now down off my roof,
     And be careful - don't fall!
You need some fresh hay
     and warm food in your stall!
Well done deer, she said,
     standing there freezin';
Her thoughts then returned
     to her efforts this season:
She had addressed all the cards
     from a mile long list;
Then received several more
     from friends she had missed!

The elves helped wrap presents
    the entire night through,
With tape on their fingers
    ribbons, paper and glue.
When she lifted her head
    and had turned it around,
She smelled something burning
    "Oh, my cookies!" she frowned.
She was chubby and plump,
    A jolly ol' soul
From testing each goodie
    and licking the bowl.

At last all was done
     by the skin of her teeth,
The mistletoe hung
     with the holly and wreath!
She had cleaned all day long
     and was covered with soot,
And her clothing was stained
     from her head to her foot.
She spoke not a word;
     she felt quite berserk;
The elves gave a sigh . . .
     She had done so much work!

She flopped on the chair,
    no breath left to whistle,
With a smile on her face
    through all she'd been blissful.
Then Santa exclaimed,
    as he left on his flight,
You're the greatest my dear!
    Merry Christmas! Good Night!

Mrs. Claus was still smiling
    as she relived these scenes
For she knew of her part
    In fulfilling our dreams.
Santa gets the credit
    though every one knows
Mrs. Claus is the hero
    who deserves hallowed prose!
So let's give a cheer for
    our own Mrs. Claus,
Her love and her work rate
    a special applause!

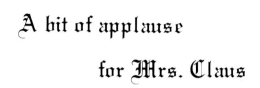

A bit of applause

for Mrs. Claus

Hip- Hip- Hooray!